I0578953

Double or Nothing
Imogene Grant

Zeta Publishing, Inc
P.O. Box 953
Silver Springs, FL 34489
www.zetapublishing.com

The views expressed in this work are solely those of the author and do not necessarily reflect the views of the publisher, and the publisher hereby disclaims any responsibility for them.

Ordering Information:
Quantity sales. Special discounts are available on quantity purchases by corporations, associations, and others. For details, contact the publisher at the address above.
Orders by U.S. trade bookstores and wholesalers. Please contact Zeta Publishing: Tel: (352) 694-2553; Fax: (352) 694-1791 or visit www.zetapublishing.com

First published by Zeta Publishing in 2021

Rev. Date: 6/1/2021

ISBN: 978-1-950340-26-2 (sc)
ISBN: 978-1-950340-27-9 (e)

Library of Congress: 2021908715
Printed in the United States of America

NARRATOR:

(Man, 40ish) sits in an easy chair near a lit fireplace facing the camera. Lou Rawls Groovy People plays softly in the back ground. The view of Sea Cliff is spectacular.

NARRATOR:

"Let me tell you a story about four guys, and two women... and The Great Turkey Baster Caper ... There is a touch of gay in the men's demeanor. They met in high school and went to the University, with full academic records, while there they organized

K.I.S.G. COMMUNICATIONS and special effects... became the news outlet on campus and parts of the town.

ROBERT SULLIVAN, Caucasian raised in a family of money, with vast interest in numerous businesses ventures... play football.

Robert has total recall seeing or hearing.

PHYLLIS MARIE STARKS, a true mixture of ethnicity Is, tall statuesque... sharp features, thick auburn hair, was always designing fashions on napkins or scraps of paper. She became the only girl in the group for a short period, her I.Q. off the charts. One would never know she is from wealth.

NARRATOR:
    LONNIE GARCIA: Smart, mostly interested in photography and cameras of all kind, he committed to memory all his friends' text books, academic scholarship to the University. His roommate was OLIVER CHAN.

    OLIVER CHAN ... Nerd extra-ordinary, computer genius, graduated in financial affairs with emphasis on world marketing. He grew up with all his needs or wants. He treated wealth with disdain, and graduated with all the knowledge of his group.

INT: SMALL OFFICE OF CHAN AND GARCIA – DAY
    Oliver says to Lonnie, "We just hit the jackpot...we have the contracts for schools in our area... for school pictures every year for the next five."
    Lonnie asked, "How did we do that?"
    Oliver replied, "I made the proposal... and we won the contract... Did you hear from Phyllis yet?"
    Lonnie said, "Yes she contacted those of us going to the University... in the fall after graduation... you remember our talks about our living quarters...Well she has been touch with us

all... we'll meet later."

They lean back and relaxed.

JOSEPH WILLINGHAM... African American
Serious, scholarly, photographic memory, the
unspoken leader of the group, his brain has no
equal... and is physically fit... due to his interest
in foods...

A serious Polo player and Captain of the
winning debate team.

Joseph is a self made multi-millionaire ... in
high school... after developing a helpful gadget
for house wives... sold for fewer than ten dollars
worldwide.

Before starting at the University Joseph
Willingham... traveled to Spain... for the final
Polo tournament matches...

Polo the horseback mounted team sports...
The game requires athletics and fair play...
Polo is scored when the ball is hit into the goal...
and the teams change field position after each
score... Joseph made the final winning goal... to
a cheering crowd...

EXT:

DUGG OUT entrance to PASSAGE WAY -
DAY Joseph on his way to the locker room...

Robert Sullivan said, "Wait up Joseph...
you remember me... Robert Sullivan... we had
classes in high school... congrats on your game
wins... "

"Thanks... I remember... you play football... also you invented... something for housewives...." Joseph replied as he mopped the sweat from his face.

Robert answered, "My team is in Spain for the last game of the season... we lost by the way... You and I have a mutual friend... Phyllis... introduced us... could we? talk over drinks after you've changed...?"

Joseph responded, "About?"

"You know Phyllis... always drawing dress fashions on scraps of paper... Well she is talking with Oliver and Lonnie from high school about us rooming together at the University... home town acquaintances... think about it." Robert said.

NARRATOR:

Robert and Joseph are roommates.

The young men while at the University read each other's text books and retained everything taken in.

The curve in their classes was ruined. As they went about their concept of the business enterprises.

With the financial help of their families. Only one thing, not overly blatant but a difference... there was a touch of gay in their demeanor.

They graduated with honors, after having created the Business' that would continue to grow... earnings off the hook and two warehouses to refurbish into their concept of the 'Village Mall' with offices and living quarters added to the roof, and two bridges to connect the structures.

Phyllis went into the business venture with the fellas... added stables for the horses... especially her favorite... Riley...

Phyllis met EDWARD ASHLEY after graduation. He is devilishly handsome and knows it. He joined the firm of ASHLEY, JOHNS, AND ASHLEY, stock brokers.

INT: ROBERTS LIVING ROOM - DAY

Phyllis dances over to him showing her engagement ring asking, "Do you just love my ring?"

ROBERT laughing said, "Hey ... who is the lucky guy?"

PHYLLIS replied saying, "Just the love of my life, Edward Ashley."

Oliver and JOSEPH enter just then.

OLIVER saying, "I heard that... You know Edward thinks he is... Gods... gift to women."

PHYLLIS answered, "He has changed... you'll see... Guys I love him."

JOSEPH smiling said, "He thinks he is all that, and he allows us... the lesser mortals to live on the planet just to do his bidding."

THREE MONTHS - THE WEDDING DAY.
LONNIE stood raises his glass, in a toast said "To Eddy and Phyl.... May they have much happiness… little Ashley's … and if you hurt Phyl I'll find a way to have you buried alive in the desert."
Edward, responded saying, "This woman is the love of my life... I wouldn't harm a hair on her beautiful head...never fear."
"A toast to the happy couple...here's to you... I'll meet you under the table later... down the hatch." Robert said.
Laughter ….
The newlyweds were off after tossing the bouquet.

INT: HONEYMOON SUITE - NIGHT
The lovers are in bed cuddle together listening to the record, FEVER.
PHYLLIS whispered, "You give me fever in the morning fever all through the night."
They fell asleep in each other's arms.

Their honeymoon was spent nearly the entire time, two weeks in the suite.

MONTAGE:
Of honeymoon activities, running on the beach, Lying in the double hammock cuddling in one another's arms... legs entwined. They

made love all over the cottage.

Toward the end of the honeymoon Edward starts to change by admiring other women.

Phyllis tried to ignore the change.

SIX YEARS LATER

INT: PARKED AUTOMOBILE - DAY

Phyllis dials the cell phone.

INTERCUT PHONE CONVERSATION:

PHYLLIS said, "Robert, he's doing it again, this is ... I don't know how many times. Today is Wednesday maids day off for his little get together."

ROBERT asked, "You have the P.I., report?"

PHYLLIS said, "In my little hot hand."

ROBERT replied, "We're all set."

PHILLIS asked, "You have the sound effect? ... I mean "EVERYTHING'?"

ROBERT replied, "Yes… everything… see you there."

EXT: HOME IN SUBURBS - AFTERNOON

K.I.S.G., News van is parked in front as a crowd of curious neighbors and other looky loo's gather.

Phyllis, a reporter and Lonnie as cameraman enter the home surreptitiously.

INT: - HALL - DAY

They walk quietly down the hall until they hear love making noises inside the bedroom... the three people entered the bedroom surreptitiously.

The sound effect makes a loud banging sound in the closed bedroom… and could be heard outside. Sprinkles of plaster sprays from the prearranged charges planted in the wall above the bed.

EXT: - LOOKY LOUS OUTSIDE - AFTERNOON

A gasp and startled whispers from the neighbors. LOOKY-LOU #1, whispered saying, "That sounds like gun fire!"

Mumbling spread through the crowd.

"That was a shot!" said LOOKY-LOU #2

A close neighbor asked, "Did she shoot him… do you suppose she shot him?"

WOMAN said, "Oh my goodness."

ONE MAN nearby, said sarcastically, "He deserved it Edward has been cheating for the last six months!"

INT: BEDROOM -DAY.

The noise frightens the naked couple they, jumped out of bed trying to cover themselves.

PHILLIS said angrily, "Edward this is the last

draw… every Wednesday, give me a break… the maid's day off. How long has this been going on?"

EDWARD stammered, saying,""Let me explain!"

PHYLLIS continued seething with anger, saying, "Your girl friend is covering herself with a pillow that I carefully selected… You brought her into our bedroom and in the bed I shared with you!"

Edward starts to dress… and the woman cowers behind a pillow.

PHYLLIS says, "No don't get dressed … and you Lady …put my pillow down, both of you leave as you are."

LONNIE (Behind camera) laughing saying, "I told you if you hurt Phyllis I would bury you. … This is better than the desert."

Another loud discharge sounds as stucco sprays from the wall over their heads.

The naked lovers ran out the bedroom door as the pistol made its third discharge above their heads in the hall… as the naked couple ran out the front door.

EXT: OUT THE FRONT DOOR - AFTERNOON
The neighbors laugh, jeer, points and applaud.

The startled couple grabbed anything to cover themselves...
Edward held a potted daisy and the naked woman tried to hide behind a watering bucket... with one arm over her bosom...
The news went viral at group gatherings every- where...

SIX WEEKS LATER.

INT: - PHYLLIS' BEDROOM - DAY
Phyllis is lying in bed, depressed and not talking to anyone.

Oliver enters… cross to the window and opens the drapes to allow the sunlight in.

Robert brings a chair… the others sit around the edge of the bed.

ROBERT said with authority, "Enough... of this… you've been in this room for six weeks and that is long enough... really... too... long."

PHYLLIS covered her eyes, grumpy saying, "Go away ... Please."   She starts to weep.

LONNIE said with concern in his voice, "No... we will not go away, we love you and we want you back... Riley needs you, too."

OLIVER added saying, "There's an encounter group... 'The Open Book.' Where you can talk everything out."

JOSEPH added firmly, "We want you to go, or we'll carry you... whatever it takes... this has to stop... now."

Phyllis tries to smile and dries her eyes. Her friends were so concerned about her unhappiness.

PHYLLIS said quietly, "I love you... too as quiet as it's kept... you had me at 'Riley' poor baby... you're so concerned about me... I'll go... I need a change from this bed. You guys are impossible but I love you... You won't go away unless I join this encounter group, right?"

OLIVER (chuckles) saying, "You were always a softy... we're as serious as a heart attack."

They laugh, hug and kiss her; all is getting better in their world again.

INT. - ENCOUNTER GROUP - NIGHT
The director addresses the group.
DIRECTOR said, "I am Josh Stoner."
The group all spoke at the same time.

GROUP says, "Hello Josh Stoner."

JOSH announced, "We are an "'Encounter Group', and are here to lend a helping hand to allow you to express your concerns...and get your life back on tract. Each of you tell us about yourself... Who will start us off?"

One young woman stood saying nervously, "I am RITA WILLIAMS."

Josh said quietly, "Don't be nervous, we are here to Listen… to you and lend a helping hand…We all have had blocks in our lives. Above all we're here to help find the best way around that block."

"My story is not new; Jerry my husband was killed six months ago. ... He was in service on night patrol. ... We were married eighteen months before he was sent into the military."

She starts to cry, Phyllis helps her to sit.

JOSH said,"We'll break for coffee."

Phyllis comforts Rita, saying, "Have a cup of coffee and we can talk later if you need to."

Phyllis crosses the room and brought two cups of coffee (saying) "My story is a little more public. ... I found my husband cheating in our home and in the bed we shared. ... Most of you probably remember seeing the spectacle plays out on public television..."

There is laughter and agreement all around.

WEEKS LATER...

'MONTAGE: of activities talks in tea rooms, walks by the lake, showing off, Rita's, accessory designs, and Phyllis' layout. Soon the sadness went from their conversations of the past to be replaced by laughter and mutual jocularity.

INT: - DINNING ROOM: - NIGHT
All are seated with RITA the new addition to the group along with an ample display of accessory designs.

PHYLLIS said, "I want my friends to meet my new best friend, Rita Williams."
ROBERT said, "We've heard a lot about you."
OLIVER said, "... And your wonderful designs... fantabulos."
He gestures toward the magnificent display, of jewelry, scarves, purses and shoes.
RITA overwhelmed, answered, "Thank you, that means a lot to me... A tear escapes from the corner of one eye, she quickly dries it away.
LONNIE saying, "That calls for a toast ..." They raise their glasses. LONNIE) cont'd) "To our new best friend and her spectacular designs."
ROBERT raised his glass, saying, "Here... here."
Everything went well for the balance of the evening, jovial conversation, hugs and inclusion

of Rita into their group.

INT: OFFICE - DAY
    Robert tosses a folder on the desk, as his three partners enter.
    LONNIE asked, "What did you find about our new best friend?"
    OLIVER said, "I'm glad you checked... Phyll hasn't been out to ride RILEY her horse for days... he misses her... you've never seen a sadder horse."
    They flop down on chairs and couch. JOSEPH laughing, "Good ole Robert never lets anything go... Okay tell us what to expect from our crying little Rita?"
    ROBERT answered, "Nothing, she is as clean as the driven snow, everything she said is true, the husband killed in action... all true."
    JOSEPH saying, "We can let out a long exhale of relief... that's a load off my mind I can't take another broken heart."
    OLIVER responded, "Now down to the business of today... remember... work."
    A serious time passes as they look at blueprints Charts... budgets and folders.
    The 'Village Mall' is a temperature controlled environment complete with its restaurants, bakeries, Phyllis' and Rita's combined Enterprises, namely DOS AMIGAS' COUTURE AND ACCESSORIES, 'b-Four' COMPLETE

WITH TELEVISION AND WORLD NEWS AND
OTHER STUDIOS, THE HOUSE OF DESIGN,
'A TOUCH OF GAY' WITH 'ANDRE AS LEAD
DESIGNER'. THE MALL SURROUNDS A
PATIO WITH SHRUBBERY AND ELABORATE
SEATING AND FOUNTAIN IN THE CENTER...
DAY CARE FOR THOSE MOTHERS WHO
NEED TO SHOP IN LEISURE, OFFICES
AND LIVING QUARTERS ADDED AT THE
TOP WITH CONFERENCE ROOMS FOR
MEETINGS.

Notification for the opening of the 'village mall'
is advertised over 'K.I.S.G. COMMUNICATION'
along with all merchandise that is available.

INT: Phyllis' OFFICE - DAY
Exasperated Phyllis answers the cell phone.
"Hello Edward!"

Intercut telephone conversation:
EDWARD said, "Hello... Phyl, can we talk?"
PHYLLIS answered saying, "Edward you
have called over seventeen times ... I have
a business to run, and a showing in seven
weeks."
EDWARD replied, "Good to know you're
counting my calls... I need to talk to you face to
face."
PHYLLIS responded, "I'll meet you at
...b-FOUR, in Thirty minutes."

She broke the connection.

EXT: THE MALL - DAY
Phyllis ambles through the park like atmosphere of the mall to b-FOUR Restaurant.

INT: The opulent b-FOUR Restaurant - DAY.
Phyllis sits and opens her mouth... starts to speak.

Edward raises his hand, saying, "Please ... let me say this before I lose my nerve ... I've lost my job. ... I've decided to go to Paris until this escapade of mine is forgotten."

PHYLLIS replied, "That will take some doing, it was funny and when you think about it ... it was very sad... uncalled for... you could have controlled your libido."

EDWRD responded, "It was your trust... What did you? expect me to do with a naked woman hiding behind me with a pillow or watering bucket? ...Should I have dropped? the flower pot, take a bow and say hi ya'll... thank ya'll for coming ... or good to see ya'll." he pauses, then chuckles, saying, "Come to think of it...that is funny." both laughed, "Thanks for the laughter...

Phyll I needed that..."   Phyllis laughing, "That's so funny. ... Just think an afternoon of anticipated sexual bliss goes so horribly wrong."

EDWARD sarcastically, "Yeah right.... You're nutty friend said he would bury me if I hurt you, and he did… only not the desert... the bastard... went overboard... buried me in giggles... finger pointing and laughter... I can't go out without a disguise. "

She said laughing, "I agree with your dad your going to Europe would be the best solution... get on with your life... the mustache helps... by the way... what happened to your girlfriend ... where is she now?"

Edward frowned then said, "I hear she left town no man would come near her...she had to wear a disguise, too."

Both laugh...

Edward asked, "Do you ever think of me? You're looking good as usual... I am sorry I put you through that."

Phyllis said, "Yes I do think of you... but, that's to be expected... You were an important part of my life for a while we had good and bad times... you grew a mustache ... it suits you... I approve."

EDWARD said, "You and father think the same... I think I'll be in Europe at least for a year ..."

PHYLLIS replied, "A good idea, really."

EDWARD saying, "It hurts ... You shot at me... three times, you're a bad shot thank goodness... scared the hell outta the girl and me... too... to be honest."

PHYLLIS said, "Don't be nutty that was just

special effects my friends Lonnie and Oliver
create every day."

EDWARD responded, "Try not to think too
badly of me. Well ... I came to say goodbye."

PHYLLIS replied, "Goodbye Eddy take care
of yourself."

NARRATOR:
THE SONG (Tomorrow Night) back ground

They part cordially. He watched her
statuesque figure, with neat waist, and flaring
hips, she seems to glide between the tables as
she tipped along on high heels.

FLASHBACK TO THEIR HONEYMOON:
As they cuddle in the double hammock, their
legs entwined, the mornings when Phyllis' lips
were slightly swollen from his kisses during their
love making. Their walks on the beach hand
and hand, her body in a string Bikini... Showers,
soapy slippery and wet... Horseback rides, and
races...

Dinner trays the food not eaten, news papers
pile outside the room, maids had to knock
several times before entering.

He untied her thin robe slipping his arms
around her soft body. He wore only a towel, her
arms around his shoulders, her head touching
his chin, and her body touches every plain of

his. They dance to the slow haunting music of Barry White for lovers. Edwards's towel falls to the floor his memory fades.

Song PLAYING IN THE BACKGROUND:
'Yesterday' ... 'All my troubles seemed so far away ... Now trouble it's here to stay.' The Music trails off in the background.
Edward shook his head sadly as her voluptuous body walks through the door. He remembers her in figure revealing gown on their honeymoon bodies touching... his arms circles her soft warm body... touching his, their kisses like nectar of the Gods as they slow dance across the room.

NARRATOR CONT'D

EXT: TEMPERATURE CONTROLLED MALL - DAY
The four men and woman ambles around the mall through the bustling crowd of shoppers, The living quarters, the offices and conference rooms, all behind a wall of glass that over look the city of Sea Cliff, California. Cross bridges connect the buildings a pleasant sight

FLASHBACK:
to the building as it grew from the necessary ground work to the necessary worker.

Bridges that connect the two buildings, and finally the glass face of the offices and living quarters plus the conference rooms.

Satisfaction is mirrored on their faces. Some shoppers sit in comfort of the sidewalk cafe and restaurant, and the patio gardens, in the coolness of the fountain in the center of the mall. While in public the group only displays a touch of Gay.

Three months later:

Invitations are sent for a formal ball to announce the opening.

EXT: OUTSIDE BALLROOM - NIGHT

The guests amble around the patio, and fountain with a spectacular view of the city of SEA CLIFF, in the background... music is heard with laughter and groups in conversation.

INT: AND EXT: BALLROOM MALL - NIGHT

The ball is in full force singing and dance music, dining, and clink of glass wear, cordial conversation as group's meanders hand and hand out the doors into the patio atmosphere of the mall.

INT: LIVING ROOM - NIGHT

Phyllis and Rita collapse into comfortable chairs.

PHYLLIS (Sips from her drink) "I needed that ... It's been one of those days."

RITA answered,, "You can say that again... I loved it... but I'm glad it's over...now I need a nap."

Weeks Later:

EXT: IN THE MALL - DAY
Phyllis and Rita sat in the coolness beside the fountain in the mall.
Families, have lunch in the park like atmosphere... Mothers push carriages...as they window shop... toddlers following mothers... fathers has babies in carry alls drooling happily...
A tear rolls down Rita's cheek, she said ."I think of my Willie...I was pregnant when he went on his last tour of duty."
Phyllis asked, "What happened?"
Rita answered, "I was notified of his death... and at the same time my parents were killed in an automobile crash... on their way here to see about me and the baby..."
Phyllis replied, " A double tragedy... You had to bare those alone... too much stress can wreak havoc on someone all at once."

More tears:
Rita dried her eyes, saying "I think about it a

lot... I wish I could have that baby...but that can't happen now."

Phyllis said, "I have wished for a child...but for a different reason...In all those years I was married... I thought I was sterile...but I had fertility tests done... I found it was probably not me...but Eddy my husband that was infertile."

"I wanted that baby... and so did Willie... I am happy he didn't live to see that our child died.. his last letter was full of what he was going to do with his son... a really happy letter..."

Phyllis said, " Maybe all is not lost... I spoke with my doctor about insemination... She said it was possible to have the insemination... you select the photo with the nearest resemblance to your husband... it's like one stop shopping.... it can tell you a lot."

Rita said, "But that's not the same."

Phyllis said, "We could give it a try... the baby would be our own to love... why don't we sleep on it? ... talk later... I can look into it with my doctor... for both of us...think about it in the mean time."

"Yes ... we'll talk later." Rita said.

They lean back comfortably to watch the tourists and other shoppers amble from store to, store some buying and some window shopping.

The construction of the Mall progresses...

Phyllis calls Rita, saying, "Don't move until I get there... I have some news for us... give me twenty minutes... tops."

Twenty minutes on the dot:
Phyllis rush in, saying, "Rita...I was in my doctors office...and spoke to several women while I waited... we talked about having babies... of course."
Rita, answered sarcastically, "That seems like an appropriate place to talk about having babies... what's your point?"
Phyllis replied, ignoring the sarcasm, "This one woman said she knew several people who got pregnant by using a turkey baster... can you imagine that?"
Rita said, "I never want what you've been drinking."
"Get this... we have four perfectly healthy young men here... they will be the donors... with no attachments... in our conversation today...it's being done safely all the time... the doctor said. " Phyllis pointed out.
Rita responded saying, "Have you lost your damn mind... if you haven't noticed lately... they're gay....don't like women."
Phyllis answered, "Don't you see...they want have relationship with us ... we will use the turkey baster to inseminate our self.... they want have interest for you or me sexually ... the

children will be ours to love and raise."

Rita showing some interest asked, "How are we going to approach them?"

Phyllis laughing, "I have a plan we'll have a party... they like parties. I'll look into it and keep you posted... think about it ... we have to do this just right like synchronize our periods within a few days... I'll check it all out... get the fellas drunk... it want be a problem... don't you just love it... the anticipation? We can have our own babies... business is great."

INT: COMPANY DINING ROOM - NIGHT
INVITATION: You are invited ...
To END OF CONSTRUCTION NIGHT...
When: Friday 8 P.M. sharp... come in a party mood...
WHERE: Executive Ballroom b-FOUR Complex...
DRESS: Elegantly Casual ...

INT: BALLROOM - NIGHT

TABLE setting for a catered affair...waiters from b-FOUR Restaurant... to serve the meal...

JOSH EVANS TRIO furnishes music to dance to...

Ms. AJA MARIE styles extraordinaire... Sings...

8 P.M. Sharp the four young men enter the

carefully breathlessly transformed ballroom ... welcomed by the music... ovation...

The Host says, "Welcome Ladies and Gentlemen to the b-FOUR Ballroom ... and the music of The JOSH EVANS TRIO... and the song styles of Ms. AJA MARIE ..

Hugs and kisses... and chatter of conversations...

To their surprise their families Moms and Dads and siblings were all assembled some sitting... the younger ones danced to the music.

All applauded...

Phyllis and Rita met them at the door...

Phyllis turns saying, "Folks the men of the hour are here."

Rita said, "Let the party begin."

Music... dancing.... singing...all from your background...

Wine served....conversation.... laughter... clinking of Glass ware toasting...

Rita announced, "Dinner is served. "

Everyone adjourns to the formal dining room... friendly chatter, laughter, through the meal... all happily tipsy.

Dinner over the families among hugs and kisses bid their farewells.

Phyllis said, "Hey guys before you leave we

have a proposition to run by you... over drinks... in the living room... while the cleanup crews are clearing the dining area... and ballroom."

They enter the living room together drinks in hand. ..

Robert asked, "What do you want to talk about?"

Phyllis responded, "We know Rita was pregnant when her husband was deployed the last time, she miscarried ... after he was killed."

Oliver sadly, "Yes we know all that... what's your point?"

Joseph added, "Are we talking about insemination... again?"

Lonnie saying, "I'm against it... not natural ... besides it's too expensive... it takes two to raise a child."

Rita replied, "I want a child to love... in memory of my husband... my Billy."

Phyllis interrupted saying, "I'm glad you brought up the expense... that brings me to our proposition... we're a family here."

Robert sips his drink saying, "Okay... now get to the nitty gritty of this insemination situation... "he paused took another sip of his drink, then said, "You saw your doctor, what did she say?"

Phyllis responded, "Dr. JUDY said we have four healthy young men friends... no sexual activity necessary... why not do it our self..."

Oliver said, "Whoa... whoa... you mean we

have to donate the sperm... you are kidding !"

Phyllis continued, "... as I was about to say... we can do the insemination our self... it's done all the time... just use sterile technique..."

Rita said, "The doctor went through the whole simple procedure... very easy... we need your input... and we have written releases you will not need to help us raise the children... with that one exception... donating your sperm."

Lonnie stood saying, "I need another drink after that... I have to think about it..."

Joseph laughing burped, saying, "I think it will work... What is there to think about... I am game... count me in... I want to see... if it'll work... come on fellas what's one little squirt... we can do it... help the girls out... give a little."

Phyllis said, "You know we will never go back on our word... our business is thriving... we can take care of the kids... and I would appreciate it... the ultimate gift... of yourselves... and then it might not work... what did we lose... think about it... nothing but a little time."

Oliver asked, "Can we do it tonight ... now that we're in the mood?... Children would be a nice idea to complete our lives..."

Phyllis saying, "I was hoping you would ask that... we have everything all set... in your bathrooms, the sterile cups with warm normal saline... wash your hands use your gloves and we're all set...."

Rita said happily, "... Even the magazines you can read while in the bathroom... put the sample in the small bag we will do the rest... and thank you... I love you madly."   Three Months Later...

INT: DR. JUDYS OFFICE - DAY

The Doctor sits across from Phyllis and Rita saying,

"Well done you both have your wish... you are both with child... we'll need sonar-grams... I will schedule them... the procedure worked... I'm surprised myself... the births should take place in about six months..."

Giggles from Rita and Phyllis...

The Doctor continues, "We'll watch your progress... I for one am happy for you... I want to see you in six weeks... these packets have your prescriptions, follow the instructions ... I want blood work before your next appointment... everything is in your packets... follow the instruction... you both are healthy you'll be fine..."

INT: b-FOURS OFFICES - EVENING

Phyllis and Rita enters... both say together, "We did it we're pregnant... due in six months... aren't you happy?"

Joseph said, " This calls for a drink... I am making strong ones... who will join me?"

They all called out... for drinks...

Robert smiling responded, "The pregnant ladies will have juice... no more drinking... and shouldn't you be sitting down?"

Phyllis happily said, "We are pregnant not dying... make mine white wine... white wine made from grapes... healthy... you dig? "

"I bow to your wisdom... just this once... from now on... you two eat and drink healthy... for our donations we have stacks in this project 'you'... dig?" Robert said.

Laughter...

NARRATER:

Three to four months... morning sickness... can't stand the odors... Rita sick from most strong odors.

Sonar-grams showed two babies each...

The men watched them do exercise suggested by doctor...

Walks around the grounds...and mat exercise...

The need of change to maternity clothes... shopping spree...

NARRATOR:

Strange food combination... like (stinky tofu)... garlic...onions...tuna fish sandwiches ...asparagus and hard boiled eggs... Kim chee to name a few...

Oliver asked, "All these late hour food runs...

don't you need to sleep for you and the babies...
Lord knows we need the rest."

NARRATAR:
   The four men... very patient...at their beck
and call at all hours...

NARRATER:
   Families curiosity at gatherings...luncheons
etc.
   Lonnie heard mother one asked, "How did
they do it the boys are gay... They don't what
girls."

   Lonnie to the other three "Mom wants to
know how the girls get pregnant?"
   Robert stood saying, "Phyllis has something
to tell you... about the babies."
   Phyllis responded saying, "We decided to
bring you up to date... Rita and I wanted a
baby... I spoke to my doctor... she gave me
the instructions... We were instructed in a do it
yourself impregnation by using a turkey baster...
to implant the male sperms."
   Stunned silence momentarily...
   Mom one asked, "Is that possible?"
   Phyllis and Rita both nods... Yes...
   Mom Two said, "If you say so dear."
   Moms... both were relieved... laughing
slapping hands with each other.

"...They got pregnant... with a Turkey
baster..." Mom one said laughing.

NARRATOR:
Phyllis' ex-husband returns from Europe:
Edward dials... the cellphone...
Intercut phone conversation:
Phyllis answers, saying, "Hello Edward... I
didn't know you were home."
Edward answered, "Hi Phyll can we talk...
meet me at b-FOUR... we need to talk... I hear
you had Riley brought to your corral... how is
he?"
Phyllis replied, "A horse by any name ...
roams around the corral... all day and eat
the day through... I'll see you in an hour at
b-FOUR."

Edward watched Phyllis walking across the
dining room... toward him... He couldn't miss
her pregnancy...
Edward surprise, saying "...Look at you... If
I had known you wanted a baby I could have
given you several."
"I am having twins... double or nothing...
loving every minute... why did you want to talk
to me?" Phyllis replied.
Edward answered, "I missed you... do you
ever think of me? I can see you haven't put
much time thinking of me..."

Phyllis responded, "Yes I think of you... as I've said before... you were an important part of my life for a while... you need to go on with yours... just as you can see my life has found a way to go on."

Edward said, "I wanted to see you... and I can see you have gone on... who is the man? "

"I am having twins... double or nothing pleases me... I have to get back I have a doctor's appointment... take care of yourself Eddy..." Phyllis answered as she exits the restaurant.

NARRATOR:
Phyllis rode Riley her spirited horse at a full gallop... on the bike path... at seven months pregnant on the mall grounds... Lonnie and Joseph... fainted... by standers bathed their faces from the fountain while others fanned them...
Robert ran frustrated said, "You better have those babies before we all have heart attacks... take it easy on us... If you need exercise we'll walk you around the complex... no more galloping around on horseback...!"
Phyllis replied out of breath happily, "Yes master."
Robert cont'd, "Rita was seen on her motor

cycle on the bike path... none of that either..."

Phyllis smiled saying, "I'll tell her...That was a great ride... Riley is comfortable like a rocking chair... only two more months... and the fun really begins..."

"No we will have nurses... on duty... and we will get some rest." Robert said.

Phyllis said, "You think?... Our agreement is valid and legally binding... you all are absolved of all responsibilities... we want hold you to them."

Robert responded, "Your famous last words... we burned those long ago... you had us at... we did it... we're pregnant... those are our samples, too..."

Phyllis answers , "You are kidding me."

Robert cont'd, "No way will we let you raise our samples... we want to see what the end product will be... 'til the bitter or glorious end we are in it to win it... you 'Dig'?" Robert replied smiling more relaxed.

THREE WEEKS LATER:

Rita awoke and sat up in bed, yelled, "Phyllis my water broke... I'm sitting in a puddle of liquid now... we're three weeks early..." the first gripping pain caused her to double over with the intensity......

Phyllis yelled back, saying "I think you're right my water broke, too... call the boys our van is gassed and ready... they can call the driver... I'll call Dr. Judy... get this show on the road." she climbed out of bed shed her wet night clothes and shrugged into her dry gown and robe.

The first baring down pain caused her to to stand and hold her abdomen.

Rita said, "I'll call for a police escort... we're... too early... we might need them... tell 'em we're having twins we're on our way to St Vincent's Emergency Room... ten blocks away..."

INT: VAN FITTED FOR TWO STRETCHERS - NIGHT

Joseph asked, "What can I do to help?"

Phyllis answered, "Who the hell cares... hold my hand I don't give a damn... I know ... peel me a grape... chew on that... damn it... this is no ride in the park it hurts like hell."

Rita said, "These pains... ain't no joke..." as another cramp gripped her saying, "Phyllis you talked me into this and I hate you for it... Oh here come another..."

Phyllis said in pain, "Shut the hell up... you came to me crying... 'I want a baby' " she mimicked Rita'..."Now you're having two... so shut the hell up, I'm having my own pains... right now"

Robert said, "If I can help... tell me what you need."

Phyllis said, "Tell the damn driver to get a move on sirens and all... where are the damn cops when you need a couple?... These kids are not waiting around..."

Joseph said. "The sirens are on... and we are nearly there... so calm down and do your breathing exercises."

Robert said calmly, "The emergency crew is waiting for us... Cling to me if you need to hold something... I am here for you both."

The delivery room... and the cries of four babies as they were born... four nurses took them wrapped in warm receiving blankets.

Joseph and Lonnie fainted during the births... the circulating nurses were ready with the smelling salts... revived them...

The mothers were cleaned... and in their room...

Rita said, "It's been quite a day... I need a nap... the children are lovely... Phyllis I didn't mean what I said..."

Phyllis said, "Ditto... it was the pain talking... I am not napping I am going to sleep the clock around... good night fellas... go see what your donations produced."

The moms fell asleep... four men tipped out... and went to the nursery to look at their children.

Names on Bassinets:

DYLAN CHAN...
Mother : Phyllis Marie Starks
Father.: OLIVER CHAN...

ANTHONY SULLIVAN ...
Mother: ... RITA WILLIAMS...
Father: Robert Sullivan...

MARISA WILLIAMS-GARCIA...
Mother: Rita Williams...
Father... Lonnie Garcia...

PRICILLA LYNN-WILLINGHAM: ...
Mother: Phyllis Marie Starks...
Father: Joseph Willingham

Hospital staff were curious but kept quiet...
as they watch the fathers look with pride at their
offspring's.
All four families converged on the hospital...
to oooo and aaahhh... and stare at the new off
springs... who slept through it all...
Home coming was a blast... well wishers...
banners...mobiles for the cribs... balloons...
Employees toasted the arrivals.
Each baby had the ancestral marker of its
fathers and mothers... One Asian... Hispanic...
African American... and Caucasian... A mixture
of ethnicities...

Each man after four months took a baby that looked like him... bought carry all for infants equiped with wet wipes and bibs for clean ups and trash bags all their needs... they walked proudly around the mall carrying the children close to their chests... as they made inspections...

The children required many clean ups...
Dylan claps to the small radio music...
Oliver says, "You like the music... enjoy... daddy does, too."
Marisa Garcia... opens she mouth showing she is cutting two teeth... she puts her little fist in her mouth...
Lonnie Garcia said, "Is my babies gums itching...?" he reaches into his bag and give his baby a cold teething ring to chew on... all the time using baby language in sweet voice.
Lonnie saying, "This will help those ole itchy gums... you'll see... yes you will... yes it will... your daddy knows exactly what to do... just chew on it sweetheart..."

Anthony drools down his chin and his bib...
Robert Sullivan, saying "Icky nasty stuff.. old dad will clean it up in no time... and I'll give you a clean one.. what do you think of that?" he take the wet bib off and changes it for a clean bib... saying, "Now... see how easy that was... all nice

and clean." Anthony smiles at him... a toothless
baby grin... daddy says... "You like that?... yes
you do."

Anthony blew more spit bubbles...
...Pricilla Lynne, given fruit finger snacks...
stuffed to much in her mouth... and threw up...
down her ruffle shirt and on her lap...
Joseph said, "That didn't agree with you...
you took too much at once... let daddy clean
you up... then I'll show you... that's what
daddies are for... to guide young ladies like
you...That's why I'm here... yes that is why I am
here..." his voice was quiet and soothing for the
baby.
Priscilla grins... and kicks her feet in the
excitement...

Fathers talks baby talk... good time had by all
... ... Children taken home with messy clothes...
... final clean ups... time for final change... nap
time... fathers like watching babies sleep ...
Phyllis asked nurse one, "Where were the
children?"
Nurse one answered, saying, "The daddies...
They came with their chest carry alls... told us to
take a break... took the kids for a walk... around
the mall and horse barn..."
Nurse number two, said "They were well
equipped with everything... wet wipes... teething

rings... fruit snacks... you know loaded for your every need... The girls wore cute little head bands, ruffled pants... the boys wore shirts and manly pants."

Phyllis dials her cell phone:

Intercuts phone conversation:

Phyllis saying, "Rita... The babies were gone... with the fathers... they took them for a walk around the mall... and horse barn... kids were dressed... with head bands, and frilly shirts... the boys in manly fashion... they told the nurses to take a break."

Rita responded..."What... you gotta be kidding... They couldn't wait 'till the kids umbilical cords healed... we might as well face it we might have to get an appointment to see our kids... they have taken over."

Phyllis answered, laughing, " I watched them through the window... when they brought them back... tired... messy and falling asleep... let's face it we've created four monsters they're as proud as could be and happy... who could have thought a turkey baster could create this much happiness ... we'll have to deal with it."

Rita answered, "You didn't mention the enormous play pen... for the babies... but the fathers are in it most... the bassinets beside them... I ask you how could you forget the huge eye sore of a play pen they constructed... for the kids... hint... hint."

Phyllis said, laughing "Yes that blew my mind...I didn't expected that... they just took over."

Rita continues, saying "We were surprised when the yards of expensive Egyptian cotton arrived... to make sheets and diapers... and the children's clothes...they said for the babies tender skin."

"You were not there when I was asked if I needed help ...expressing milk for the kids... you know they researched the machines before they decided...and ordered those expressing machines for our milk..." Phyllis said.

Rita replied, "As if we needed help... they're going a bit far."

Phyllis answered, "The kids have their own radios... And the music plays... from all cultures constantly... and there are the music instruments... for kids that will only drool on them now... it's as I have said we've created four picky monsters."

Hangs up laughing.

INT: GIANT PLAY PEN- NURSERY-DAY
The children are beginning to crawl all moving in different ways.... stands with his head down... rocking on the abdomen... climbs one fathers leg... try to stand and falls... sucking on pacifiers... they can find the smallest fibers or

tooth picks... and taste everything they find...
and taste... evening comes with sleep time the
fathers looks at the sleeping children.

The play pen floor covering is changed daily...
with a laundered cover...

Nurse one cautioned... "Be sure and burp the
children after a bottle if you have, too... do it the
way we showed you."

Oliver said, "I'll be fine the kids are sleeping
what can go wrong? ... A piece of cake... I've
got this covered... have a nice break."

"Your colleagues are in the mall... you can get
us by our cellphone... and them too. "said nurse
two.

The nurses leave...Oliver settles down to
read papers.... Dylan was asleep on his chest...
throws up ...Oliver feels the warm milk run down
his neck into his arm pit and back...

Pricilla and the other two starts to cry...

Oliver panics... lost the cellphone in the
covers... while holding the baby... he tries to
settle Dylan down... finally... the child's diaper
falls off... Oliver had forgotten to fasten it...

Dylan peed in Oliver's expensive loafers and
down his trousers legs...

Oliver retrieves the cellphone... babies crying
still...

He yells saying, "Help!... All hell is loose
here they're all awake and crying... bring the

nurses... quick !"

Oliver was a sight... clothes soaked with formula... trousers and shoes wet from baby urine... the nurses and men entered to his frustrated and disheveled sight.

Nurses went to work quieting everything.

Oliver said, "After all my frustration...and the ruin of my favorite loafers... Dylan had the sweetest toothless smile... it was worth it... melts your heart... I've reached the conclusion... the nurses need a raise... right away... along with a bonus."

Six months: feeds and bathes kids...

Breakfast: Bacon, eggs, toast, juice, fresh fruit...

Priscilla throws up...with too much food in her mouth... the nurse quickly... cleans the child's face.... and helps by adding more milk and cutting the morsels smaller.

Dylan spits milk on high chair tray...and splash his hands in the puddle...

Marisa... dumps her milk and cornflakes on the floor and watch over the edge of the highchair as it spreads on the floor...

Anthony sips his juice then pours milk and spits juice over the edge and laughs as it runs down his legs and drips in his shoes... splashed on the floor...

The children finished with breakfast were stripped and starts their bath...

they loved splashing in the water, getting the fathers wet...

some shoves the rubber duckies around... and other bath toys...

soap in hair and eyes...splashing...

EIGHTEEN MONTHS OF AGE

... nurses day off...fun A cacophony of noises...

Children begins... crawling around the playpen...

standing... dancing by stamping their feet in place... ...banging piano board... walking unsteadily sitting down abruptly...

... each child has a radio changing stations... drum beats... parents want to observe how the children play and interact... together...

Anthony pours milk on Marisa's food tray... ... Marisa chews on a strip of bacon... with her four teeth...

Anthony cuts chunks of Marisa's hair...she laughs'...

The mother not amused, asked, "Is that the hair style you wanted dear? Is that your fashion statement today...?"

"My brother did it." Marisa hugged him.

Dylan squeezes soap foam... and watch

it ooze through his... fingers... then licks his hands... that didn't taste good... he makes a face and spit the foam out...

The children at different stages of walking...

Pricilla falls down cries tear down one cheek, saying, "Fall down on my but can we have a big hug?" she rubs her fanny.

Grandparents come bearing gifts... after finding how the children were conceived...

The kids were introduced to fried chicken drumsticks...they sucked and slobbered grease and drooled as it oozes between their fingers... they enjoyed the first fried food... as they moved rhythmically in their high chairs... each had few teeth.

Each father were appalled because the children were off their well balanced diets...was shot....

The children never differentiated with the grandparents nor the uncles, aunts and cousins.... there were kisses, dancing and adulation... then the kids treated everyone to a big group hug.

INT: LIVING ROOM – Night
NARRATOR:

You will want to know what happened to the children.

A MONTAGE OF GROWING UP:
Musical Jam Sessions...singing...dancing... learning enjoying life and irritating their siblings...

PRICILLA LYNNE ...statuesque beauty a "Powers Model"... She captured the modeling stage...as a pubescent child star of the runway... and has been in demand from day one...

Shows a film short...of Pricilla as she pirouette in place... into a provocative pose...

MARISA GARCIA...An entertainer... sings the blues... dancer on the stage and screen... throughout the world...

She is photographed beside the Arch of Triumph...

Anthony athlete... excelled in Polo... a dabbler in herbal medicines... he discovered treatments for numerous health issues... Concert quality Pianist... loves Jazz...

Dylan Chan interests includes innovations in the development of cameras... as it applied to special effects and their many uses...in industry... movies...and security in business... homes and other safety measures

Tonight we will be entertained by the children and friends musical talents... An old fashion "JAM SESSION" There you have my story of four brilliant young men with a touch of ...GAY...

"The two young mothers who tolerated it all...

good night for now...ENJOY."

The music swells as the Narrator settled back with his drink and pipe to listen... and enjoy an old fashion ' toe tapping 'JAM SESSION' .

THE END:

WRITER: IMOGENE GRANT PAGES: 54
WORDS: 8.048

www.ingramcontent.com/pod-product-compliance
Lightning Source LLC
Chambersburg PA
CBHW030824200726
48288CB00004B/1390